THE TRIGGLE

WRITTEN BY
JOSEPHINE SMITH-MANDS

For Skitz.
Being at my side every step of the way and being the
most amazing husband and dad to our three boys

Published in association with Bear With Us Productions

ISBN: 978-1-5272-9493-6

Design by Luisa Moschetti

www.justbearwithus.com

ILLUSTRATED BY
Matt Riste

THE TRIGGLE

WRITTEN BY
Josephine Smith-Mands

Meet the Sniggles.
Everyone has Sniggles.

The Sniggles are in charge of carrying around your emotions.

HAPPY

ANGER

FEAR

DISGUST

SAD

MEET SMUDGE.
EVERYONE HAS A SMUDGE.

SMUDGE IS LIKE A COMPUTER IN YOUR BRAIN. HIS JOB IS TO REMIND YOU AND THE SNIGGLES, HOW WORRIES HAVE BEEN DEALT WITH IN THE PAST.

MEET THE TRIGGLE.
EVERYONE HAS MET THE TRIGGLE.

HE CAN BE TRIGGERED BY SOUNDS, SIGHTS, SMELLS, TEXTURES AND TASTES. HE CAN CAUSE BIG WORRIES FOR THE SNIGGLES AND YOU. HE LOVES TO CREATE CHAOS!

Peter was afraid of the Triggle; they were not friends.

The Triggle lurked everywhere and was very naughty. It caused Peter BIG WORRIES.

The Triggle didn't like lots of things, and could create all kinds of chaos from minor upsets to angry meltdowns if it came across something that it didn't like.

When the Triggle was triggered, it embarrassed Peter.

One day, Peter was in the supermarket with Mum.

Peter was worried, the Triggle always
appeared on supermarket days.

As Mum looked at flowers, Peter noticed
the flickering of the lights above.
He knew this provoked the Triggle.

Mum placed a flowerpot into the trolley.
It sounded like a noisy train squeaking and
scratching, this irritated the Triggle.

Mum knew that Peter was getting anxious.

Peter was worried.

In a flash...
The Triggle crept inside Peter's nose,

MAKING THE FLOWERS SMELL DISGUSTING.
"THEY STINK!" SHOUTED PETER.

"Everything will be OK."

Mum reassured him, taking away the flower pot.
She knew the Triggle was causing a problem.

As Mum pushed the trolley away from the flowers, the Triggle flew inside Peter's ear.

Peter lashed out at Mum.

"It's too LOUD!" he yelled.

"Calm down," said Mum softly.

FURIOUS, PETER RAN AWAY. MUM RAN AFTER HIM,
DOWN EVERY AISLE AROUND THE SUPERMARKET.

When she caught up, Mum hugged Peter close. They sat together on the floor. People stared at them. "Stop being a naughty boy for your Mum," said one of the people who were staring.

These people made Peter sad.
The dark cloud that hung over his head grew darker, he felt like he couldn't breathe.

"It's OK, you aren't naughty."
Mum held Peter tightly and reassured him, wishing people wouldn't stare or say unhelpful things.

Peter became VERY overwhelmed with his emotions. Suddenly, the Triggle smashed into his eyes, making everything blurry.

THE PEOPLE WHO WERE STARING DIDN'T LOOK LIKE
PEOPLE ANYMORE, AND MUM DIDN'T LOOK LIKE MUM.

Peter jumped up and ran.

Mum started her chase again.

"Can I help?" a lovely lady who worked
in the supermarket offered.

"Yes, please make sure someone is at the exit door so
Peter doesn't run into the car park,"
Mum replied, worried that this could get dangerous.

It was chaos as Mum and the lady ran from aisle to aisle. As Peter ran for the door, Mum finally caught up with him.

THE TRIGGLE HAD COMPLETELY TAKEN OVER, AND PETER
WAS SOMEWHERE RUNNING AROUND IN HIS MIND,
VERY LOST, VERY CONFUSED AND VERY FRIGHTENED.

Mum struggled with Peter until she managed to stop him running around in his mind and focus on her whilst they got to a safe place.

They sat on a bench in a quiet area of the carpark.

Mum looked bedraggled.

Strangers had gathered around
and were staring at them.

Peter's screams got worse because there
were too many faces and voices again

"EVERYONE, PLEASE LEAVE THEM ALONE," THE KIND LADY STARTED TO MOVE THE CROWD AWAY FROM MUM AND PETER. SHE EVEN ASKED ANOTHER MEMBER OF STAFF TO GET SOME WATER, A COMIC AND SOME SWEETIES FOR PETER.

BUT...

The Triggle was still lurking.

"MY TOES!" Peter screamed, beginning
to jump up and down.

"What's happening?" asked Mum.

"Tingles in my toes!" Peter cried.

Mum stopped Peter from bumping into cars.
She hugged him and helped him sit down on the bench.
The kind lady had bought Peter some bubbles.

She sat next to Mum and began
blowing the bubbles in the air.

Peter peeked out from behind Mum, watching
as the bubbles floated gently towards him.

He smiled.

It felt nice and calm; he wasn't worried about the Triggle anymore.

Peter was safe sitting on the bench with Mum and the kind lady.

Peter felt something moving around in his head. It was a bit creaky up there, but he knew it wasn't the Triggle.

"Hello, Peter," said a voice.

Peter looked at Mum, that voice
didn't sound like her.

"Can you hear me?" asked the voice.

Peter nodded.

Hello, Peter,

Can you hear Me?

"My name is Smudge; I live inside your brain. I get sent messages to me so I help you manage with everything that is going on," Smudge explained. "I captured the Triggle by trapping him inside your toes. That's why you felt them tingling. It's exhausting work trying to train the Triggle."

Peter listened.

"I need some help training him. You will need to help me. I know you can do it." Smudge continued, "By staying calm and focusing on the nice things like those big bubbles, you will help train him."

"But what if he comes back?" asked Peter.

"You can trap him inside your toes!
You can train him to be a better Triggle,"
said Smudge.

"But what if I still can't do it?" said Peter.

"Then I will chase him into your toes," Smudge replied.

Peter smiled.
It sounded like a good plan.

THE NOISES AND SMELLS HAD GONE, HE COULD SEE
AGAIN AND HIS BODY DIDN'T FEEL WOBBLY AT ALL.

HE FELT HAPPY, HIS WORRIES HAD GONE.
DAD ARRIVED TO GET MUM AND PETER.

But first, they had a mission to complete. Dad and Peter went back into the supermarket and headed for the flowers.

Peter picked a flowerpot himself and put it into the trolley, it smelt lovely and was very colourful.

Everything looked so different now,
in a good way.

Outside, Peter handed Mum the
flowerpot and she smiled.

Today was a good day after all.

These days, Peter spends most of his time training his Triggle in various places.

When it doesn't work out, Smudge reminds him to wiggle his toes. That usually helps.

About the author

Josephine loves writing books for everyone.
Her mission is to write stories that make the world a better place and to highlight subject matters, which some might find difficult to speak about. She believes it is essential to create stories that stir the imagination, touch the heart, inspire, and mostly sprinkle happiness and hope to those who read them.

Josephine is the wife of her best friend and has three sons.
She is a psychotherapist in higher psychotherapy and holds a diploma in child psychology.

In her spare time, Josephine loves family time and enjoys walking in the woods; she also enjoys spending time on her family boat, where she often can be found speaking to the ducks on the River Thames

Printed in Great Britain
by Amazon